50

Happy Birthday Bugs

Bugs 50th logo is a trademark of Warner Bros. Inc. © 1990

This Looney Tunes Library Book is published by Longmeadow Press
in association with Sammis Publishing.
Distributed by Book Sales, Inc., 110 Enterprise Ave.,
Secaucus, NJ 07904

With special thanks to

Guy Gilchrist • Jim Bresnahan • Mike Favata • Frank McLaughlin • Tom Brenner
Mary Gilchrist • Mike Micinillio • Rich Montasanto • John Cacanindin
Allan Mogel • Gary A. Lewis

Printed in the United States of America
0 9 8 7 6 5 4 3 2 1

DON'T JUST SIT THERE SPACE CADET, HELP ME FIND A PARKING SPACE!
AYE-AYE, YOUR CAPTAINSHIP!

DAFFY DUCK *and* PORKY PIG *in*
DUCK DODGERS *in* OUTER SPACE

written by Gary A. Lewis

Illustrated by
The *Guy Gilchrist* Studios
™

Far, far, far, far, far, far, far, far, far, far, far, far, far, far, far in the future, in a galaxy far, far, far, far, far, far, far, far, far, far—

To continue…far, far, far, far, far away lived the greatest spacefaring hero the universe has ever known—Duck Dodgers in the 24½th Century!

Duck's constant and faithful companion was Space Cadet First Class Porky Pig.

AH-CHOOO!

Duck Dodgers and Space Cadet Porky had visited all twenty-three moons of the planet Jujube. They had lived through the ice storms of Coldius and the firestorms of Hottius. Together, they had shared many a hair-raising adventure.

THAT'S HAIR RAISING NOT HARE RAISING.

So come with us as we follow the adventures of…Duck Dodgers and Space Cadet Porky Pig…in the 24½th Century!

Dr. I.Q. Hi, Secretary of the Stratosphere, had a crisis of megatonic proportions on his hands. The world's supply of aludium fozdex, the shaving cream atom, was alarmingly low. And aludium fozdex could only be found on the mysterious Planet X.

"Are you ready to save the Earth from a shaving cream shortage, Duck Dodgers?" Dr. Hi asked Duck.

"Of course, sir," Duck responded. He turned to Porky. "Are you ready to save the Earth from a shaving cream shortage, eager young space cadet?"

"I'm reh-reh-reh—all set, your heroship, sir," the young cadet replied.

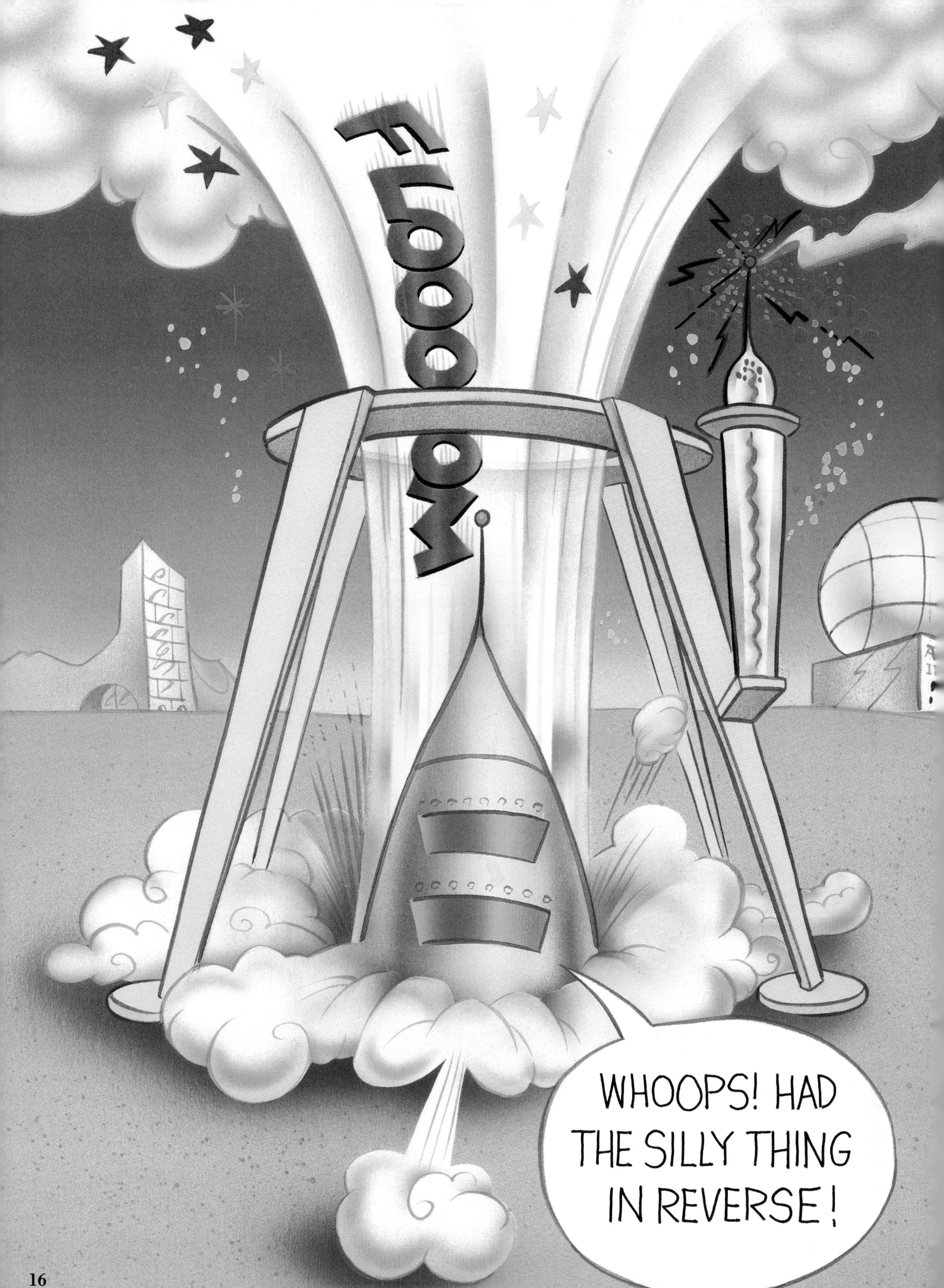
FLOOOOOM
WHOOPS! HAD THE SILLY THING IN REVERSE!

17

Duck Dodgers had been trained to find his way around space with ease. He plotted a clever course that would take them only three billion trillion zillion miles away from Planet X. No one had ever gotten this close to the mysterious planet before.

"This is the course we'll take to reach Planet X," Duck Dodgers explained to Space Cadet Porky. "Starting from where we are, we go 36,320 turbomiles due up, then west in an astro-arc deviation to here. Then, following the great radial loop, we'll go south by northeast, by astro-astroble to here, then by space navigal compass to here, making sure we go thirteen points due sideways, and finally traveling four million light years to our destination."

ACME SCIENCE-FICTION PROP

Luckily, while Duck was plotting their course, Space Cadet Porky happened to notice something mysterious about the galaxy they were traveling in. The planets were all named for letters of the alphabet.

"You see, sir?" Porky explained. "All we have to do is follow the planets marked A through W, and we can't miss Planet X."

"I'm certainly glad I noticed that," said Duck Dodgers.

Using this clever navigating device, Duck Dodgers and Space Cadet Porky managed to locate Planet X. Once they had landed, Duck wasted no time in staking his claim to the aludium fozdex on the planet.

"I hereby plant this flag and claim Planet X in the name of Earth!" said Duck.

Duck was just planting the flag when a large, menacing, alien spaceship flew overhead. Somebody else obviously intended to claim Planet X, too!

And that somebody was…a Martian! Marvin the Martian!

"I hereby claim this planet in the name of Mars!" the Martian said.

"Listen, you Martian, you," Duck bravely replied. "I just claimed this planet for Earth. And there isn't room on it for the both of us."

"You're right," the Martian agreed. "There *isn't* room on this planet for the both of us."

Duck tried to reason with the Martian, but it was no use. The Martian was clearly not interested in giving up Planet X. In fact, the Martian was so disinterested in giving up Planet X that he pulled out his disintegrating ray gun to prove it.

So Duck retreated to his spaceship to figure out what to do.

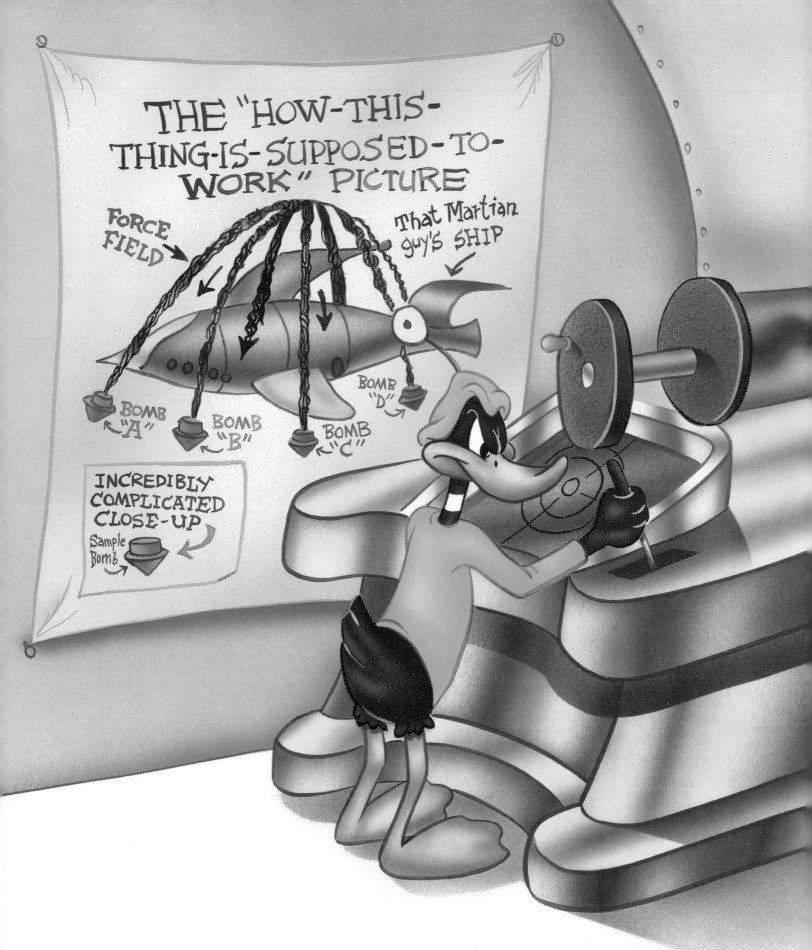

After consulting with Space Cadet Porky, Duck decided that the only way to defeat the Martian and win Planet X was to use his Very Top-Top-Secret Weapon. He had purchased it at the Acme Discount Secret Weapons Emporium, located on a small asteroid just outside the Milky Way.

"It looks complicated, sir," said Space Cadet Porky.

"Nothing complicated about it," said Duck. "It says here in the instructions that you simply line up the telescopically superior hypersight, making sure the hypervector is in the seventy-degree slightly upright position before putting your index digit over the protuberance on the dashboard and employing a field of vector two point zero. Now do you know how to fire one of these things?"

"Sure," said Space Cadet Porky. "You just aim it and then push that button over there."

Unfortunately, what Duck Dodgers didn't know was that the Martian shopped at the Acme Discount Secret Weapons Emporium, too. And he had recently purchased the same secret weapon when it was on sale.

Just as Porky pushed the button, the Martian fired *his* Very Top-Top-Secret Weapon. In a minute, both spaceships were enveloped by a deadly force field.

ZAP

Y-Y-Y-ALL RIGHT, SIR!

FIRE!

30

In another moment, both spaceships were rocked by giant explosions. It seemed as if the entire planet would be destroyed!

The smoke slowly cleared. Who would be left to claim Planet X? Who would win the battle? Who would capture all the aludium fozdex? Would it be the evil Martian or Duck Dodgers? Who would it be? Who? Who?

OH, COME ON! TELL THEM ALREADY!

Duck Dodgers in the 24½th Century…
that's who!
  Duck stood on what was left of Planet X.
"As I was saying, buster," he said, "this
planet isn't big enough for the both of us!"
  "Yeeeiiiikes!" the Martian agreed.

34

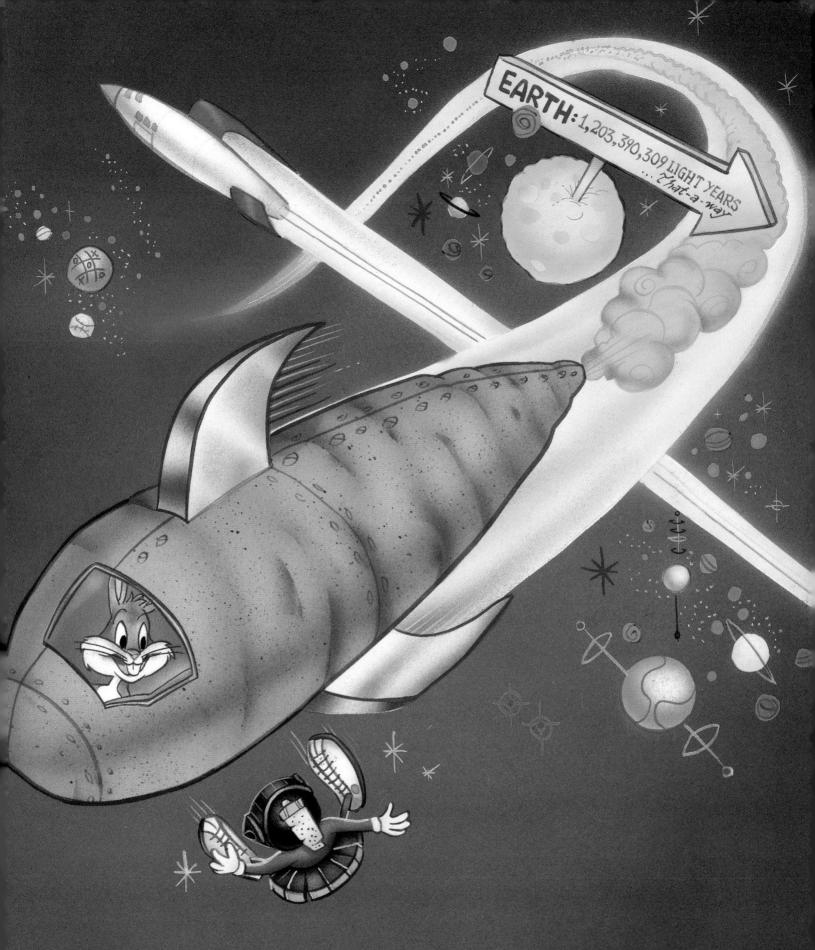

After claiming Planet X in the name of Earth, Duck Dodgers collected the alludium fozdex that was left after the explosions—there was about one teaspoon of it—and headed home once again, secure in the knowledge that he had saved his planet from destruction.

His mission accomplished, Duck Dodgers thought he'd take a nice little vacation.
But before too long, Duty Called.

Once more, Duck Dodgers in the 24½th Century was on his way to another great adventure…to save the planet Earth from destruction.

Duck Dodgers and Space Cadet First Class Porky were on their way to Mars. The Secretary of the Stratosphere had received a warning that Martians were about to launch an attack on Earth.

MARS
that-a-way!!

When Duck and Porky landed on Mars, they decided to lie low for awhile and see what they could discover.

It was lucky they did…because they soon stumbled onto the Martian. And he was obviously up to no good.

Luckily, the Martian didn't notice them, so Duck Dodgers and Space Cadet Porky were able to follow him to his secret weapon.

"At last!" he muttered to himself. "The most important part of my aludium Q36 explosive space modulator is ready. Now to blow up Earth!"

But why would the Martian want to blow up Earth?

The Martian's secret weapon was the ever-popular aludium Q36 explosive space modulator, purchased for only $9.95 at the Acme Discount Secret Weapons Emporium (batteries not included).

The aludium Q36 explosive space modulator had the power to blow up all the planets in the universe. And it was pointed straight at Earth!

But before the Martian could blow up anything, Duck acted. Cleverly removing the most important part of the aludium Q36 explosive space modulator, he raced off with it.

"Where's the kaboom?" the Martian said. "There was supposed to be an Earth-shattering kaboom!"

But the aludium Q36 explosive space modulator was safe in the hands of Duck Dodgers!

WHOOPS!

The Martian looked everywhere for his aludium Q36 explosive space modulator. Finally, he figured out what had happened.

"That creature has stolen the space modulator!" he cried. "I must get it back so that I can restore my view and make sure that Martian property values don't go down!"

Quickly, the Martian pulled out a jar of 10,000 instant Martians and started adding water. A quick stir, and he had an entire army at his command.

"After them!" he commanded. "They've stolen the space modulator!"

Duck and Space Cadet Porky were outnumbered by angry Martians. It didn't look good for our heroes. But then Duck Dodgers came up with a clever plan.

When they had disposed of most of the Martians, Duck Dodgers and Porky raced for the spaceport. They had to find a way to get off of Mars in a hurry.

And find a way they did...getting rid of the aludium Q36 explosive space modulator at the same time.

And it was lucky they did—because the aludium Q36 explosive space modulator was about to explode!

And so, Duck Dodgers in the 24½th century once again managed to defeat the enemy—saving the planet Earth and making the galaxy safe from Martians with aludium Q36 explosive space modulators.